Please return this book on or before the date shown
above. To renew go to www.essex.gov.uk/libraries,
ring 0845 603 7628 or go to any Essex library.

DS12 4005

Essex County Council

ELMER AND THE HIPPOS
A RED FOX BOOK 978 0 099 45114 3 (from January 2007)
0 099 45114 X
First published in Great Britain by Andersen Press Ltd

Andersen Press edition published 2003
Red Fox edition published 2004

3 5 7 9 10 8 6 4

Copyright © David McKee, 2003

Red Fox Books are published by Random House Children's Books,
61–63 Uxbridge Road, London W5 5SA,
a division of The Random House Group Ltd,
in Australia by Random House Australia (Pty) Ltd,
20 Alfred Street, Milsons Point, Sydney, NSW 2061, Australia,
in New Zealand by Random House New Zealand Ltd,
18 Poland Road, Glenfield, Auckland 10, New Zealand,
and in South Africa by Random House (Pty) Ltd,
Isle of Houghton,Corner of Boundary Road & Carse O'Gowrie,Houghton 2198,South Africa

THE RANDOM HOUSE GROUP Limited Reg. No. 954009
www.kidsatrandomhouse.co.uk

A CIP catalogue record for this book is available from the British Library.

Printed in China

ELMER
and the HIPPOS

David McKee

RED FOX

Elmer, the patchwork elephant, was having a friendly chat with Lion and Tiger when three angry elephants came by.

"Elmer," said one, "the hippos have come to live here."

"Tell them to go, Elmer," said the second. "There isn't room for them and us."

"What if they don't want to go?" asked Elmer.

"Tell them we'll make them," said the third elephant.

"Hmmm," said Elmer. "Let me talk to them."

"Hello, Hippos," said Elmer.

"Hello, Elmer," said the hippos.

"Elmer," said one, "we know we're not wanted here but our river has dried up and we have to have a river."

"Make yourself at home," said Elmer. "I'll speak to the elephants."

Elmer told the elephants the hippos' problem.
"Imagine if our river dried up," he said.
The elephants agreed to let the hippos stay,
but grumbled because the river would be crowded.
"I'll take a look at their river," said Elmer.

The hippos' river was completely dry.
"Strange," thought Elmer. "I wonder what's happened?"
He set off along the dry river bed.

At last he came to some cliffs. The gap where the river normally flowed was blocked by a pile of rocks.

"The rocks fell and stopped the river," a bird said.

"Move the rocks and the river will flow again," thought Elmer. "But that means a lot of work."

On his way home, Elmer visited his cousin, Wilbur.
"Come on, Wilbur," he said. "I need your help."

"Good," said the elephants when they heard the news. "The hippos can move the rocks, get their river back and go home."

"It will take them ages," said Wilbur. "They don't have trunks. Still, they can stay here and use our river."

An elephant said, "If we help it will soon be done."

"Right," said Elmer. "Get a good night's sleep. We'll start early in the morning."

The next morning, Elmer called the hippos.
"Come on, we're going to get your river back.
Are you feeling strong?"

The elephants and hippos were soon bragging about how strong they were as they marched along.

When they saw the rocks, the bragging
stopped and they set to work,
pushing and pulling them from the gap.
   As the pile became smaller, they all
became dustier.
   "I'd love a nice dip in the river now,"
said an elephant.
   "Keep working and you'll soon be able to,"
laughed Elmer.

Some time later, a hippo shouted,
"Water!" as the first trickle came
through the rocks.
"Careful," said Wilbur.
"It will come with a rush."

It did.
The water suddenly poured through, pushing the last
of the rocks out of the way.

Cheering and laughing, they all plunged into the river
and forgot their tiredness as they washed off the dust and
played in the water.

When they finally parted, the hippos thanked the elephants and said, "Come and visit us any time."

"You too," said the elephants. "Any time!"

Later, Elmer said, "You were all pretty friendly with the hippos in the end."

"Of course," said an elephant. "Besides, imagine if our river dried up?"

Other titles you might enjoy:

GEORGE AND THE DRAGON
Chris Wormell

YOU DO!
Kes Gray and Nick Sharratt

HAPPY!
Caroline Castle and Sam Childs

ANNIE ROSE IS MY LITTLE SISTER
Shirley Hughes

ERIC THE RED
Caroline Glicksman

SPLASH!
Jane Hissey

FRIENDS TOGETHER
Rob Lewis

TANKA TANKA SKUNK!
Steve Webb